T0401301

SUPERHUMAN MEMORY

Jessica Rusick

Big Buddy Books
An Imprint of Abdo Publishing
abdobooks.com

abdobooks.com

Published by Abdo Publishing, a division of ABDO, PO Box 398166, Minneapolis, Minnesota 55439.

Printed in the United States of America, North Mankato, Minnesota
102021
012022

Design: Emily O'Malley, Mighty Media, Inc.
Production: Mighty Media, Inc.
Editor: Rebecca Felix
Cover Photographs: Shutterstock Images
Interior Photographs: Karjean Levine/Getty Images, p. 15; Lucio Scatola/Wikimedia, p. 5; Marius Becker/AP Images, p. 25; Shutterstock Images, pp. 7, 9, 11, 13, 17, 19, 21, 21 (all), 22, 27, 29 (all); Sipa USA/AP Images, p. 23
Design Elements: Shutterstock Images

Library of Congress Control Number: 2021942816

Publisher's Cataloging-in-Publication Data
Names: Rusick, Jessica, author.
Title: Superhuman memory / by Jessica Rusick
Description: Minneapolis, Minnesota : Abdo Publishing, 2022 | Series: Superhuman science | Includes online resources and index.
Identifiers: ISBN 9781532197024 (lib. bdg.) | ISBN 9781644947180 (pbk.) | ISBN 9781098219154 (ebook)
Subjects: LCSH: Human physiology--Juvenile literature. | Performance--Juvenile literature. | Ability--Juvenile literature. | Memory--Juvenile literature. | Photographic memory--Juvenile literature. | Super powers--Juvenile literature.
Classification: DDC 599.9--dc23

DON'T TRY THIS AT HOME

Many of the superhuman feats described in this series were overseen by trainers and doctors. Do not attempt to re-create these feats. Doing so could cause injury.

CONTENTS

AMAZING ABILITY

Superheroes have superpowers. But real men and women also have **amazing** abilities. Some people have superhuman memory!

Many people with superhuman memory compete at events. Andrea Muzii won the 2019 IAM World Memory Championship. He memorized 572 numbers in 5 minutes!

WHAT IS MEMORY?

Memory has three parts. First, your brain takes in **information**. Then, it stores the information. You can later remember the information. Memory is how we think back on our lives, solve problems, and learn new things!

Playing matching games can help strengthen your memory.

MAKING A MEMORY

Imagine you are at a birthday party. You see balloons and taste cake. These senses send electrical **signals** through your brain cells. The signals connect some cells together in a pattern. This pattern is a memory!

When you think back on a past event, it reactivates the same cell pattern as when the memory was made.

SHORT & LONG

Our brains store some memories longer than others. Short-term memories are things we remember for 20 to 30 seconds. We forget many of these memories. Others become long-term memories. These are things we remember for days, weeks, or years.

Looking at photos can help reactivate long-term memories.

MAGIC MEMORY

There are two types of long-term memory. Implicit memories are things we remember without thinking. Explicit memories are things we must recall. These include events. We often form stronger memories of events that are important to us.

Tying your shoes is an example of an implicit memory. Once you learn how to do it, you remember how to do it without thinking.

Most people forget everyday events soon after they happen. But not American Jill Price! She can remember her life in **extreme detail**. This **rare** ability is called hyperthymesia. Price can remember exactly what she did on most days of her life.

SMALL GROUP

Scientists know of fewer than 100 people with hyperthymesia.

Jill Price remembers details of every day of her life since she was 14 years old!

GROWING MEMORY

Some people are born with superhuman memory. Others get their abilities through practice. London, England, has 25,000 streets. London's taxi drivers must memorize them all!

TRAINING TIME

A London taxi driver's training takes years.

London taxi drivers must also memorize all the city's landmarks. This includes every park, shop, and more!

Scientists studied London taxi drivers as they trained. Over time, memorizing **information** changed the drivers' brains! The hippocampi are parts of the brain that help form and store long-term memories. Drivers had average-sized hippocampi before training. Their hippocampi were larger after training.

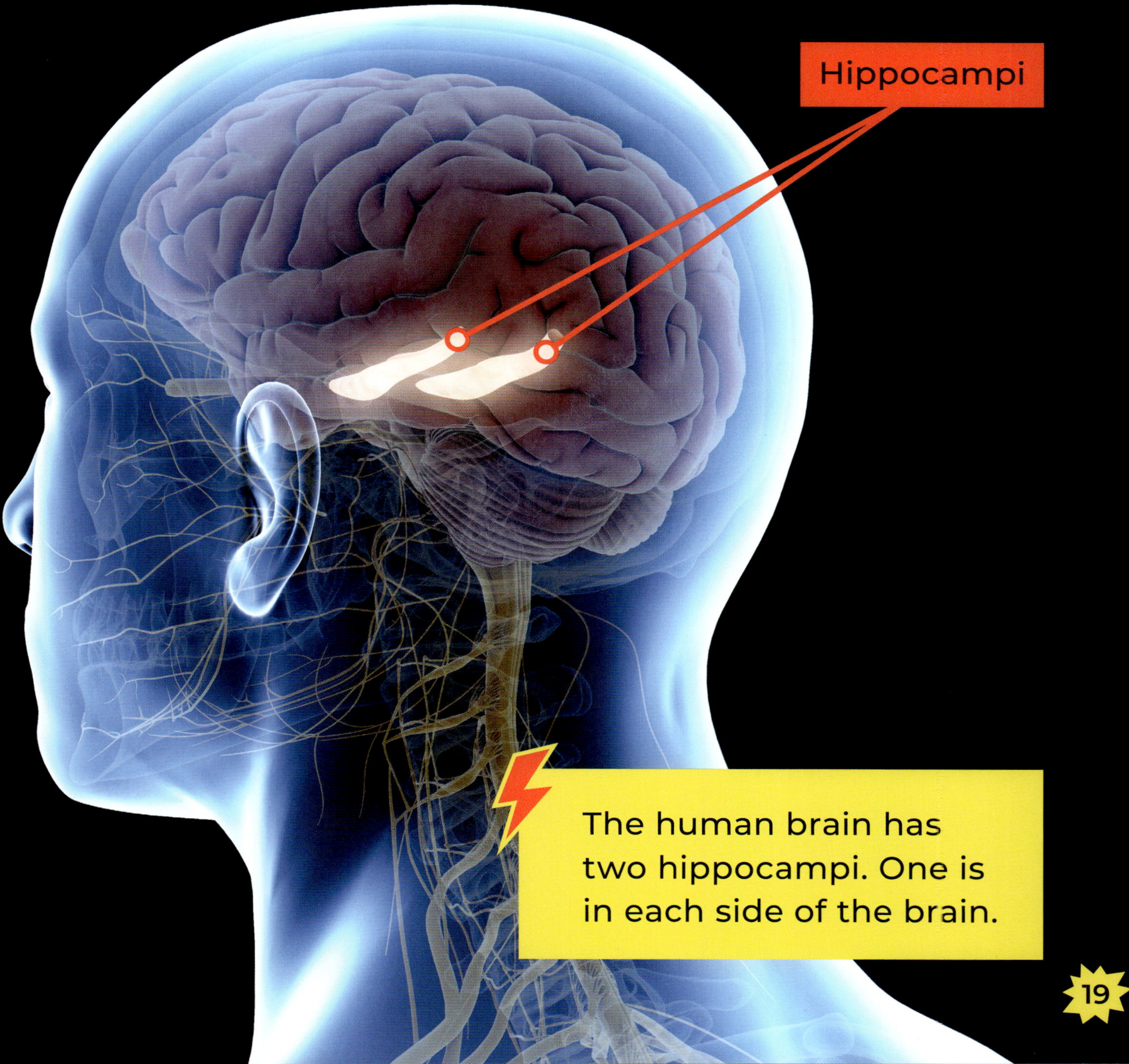

The human brain has two hippocampi. One is in each side of the brain.

IMAGE MEMORY

Some people remember **information** using memory tricks. One trick is to turn words into images. Images spark more memory-related activity in the brain than words do. So, we remember images better than words.

When using images to memorize words, including color and detail makes stronger connections in the brain.

Mongolian-Swedish Yanjaa Wintersoul is a memory **athlete**. She **competes** in memory contests. Wintersoul memorizes long lists of words by creating silly images. For example, if the word *cow* follows the word *ball*, she might picture a cow playing basketball!

Yanjaa Wintersoul believes anyone can improve their memory. She said, “The more you try to remember, the more you will remember.”

MEMORY PALACE

Another memory trick combines images and places together. It is called the memory palace. German Boris Konrad is a memory **athlete**. He once memorized 201 names in 15 minutes! Konrad often uses the memory palace trick.

Boris Konrad prepares to solve a Rubik's Cube blindfolded on television in 2014.

First, Konrad turns **information** into images. Then, he imagines a place he knows well. This is his memory palace. Konrad places the images along a path through the palace. He imagines himself walking the path. The path helps him remember the images. And the images help him remember the original information!

ANCIENT TRICK

People have used the memory palace trick for thousands of years.

Any location you know well can become a memory palace. This could be a favorite park, hallways at your school, or even your bedroom!

BUILD A MEMORY PALACE

Want to improve your memory? Build a memory palace!

1. Pick a place you know well, such as your bedroom.
2. Imagine a path through your chosen place. Think of six locations where you will stop.

3. Connect one of the words below to each stop. Maybe you imagine a duck snoring in your bed!

duck, crayon, umbrella, apple, flower, shoes

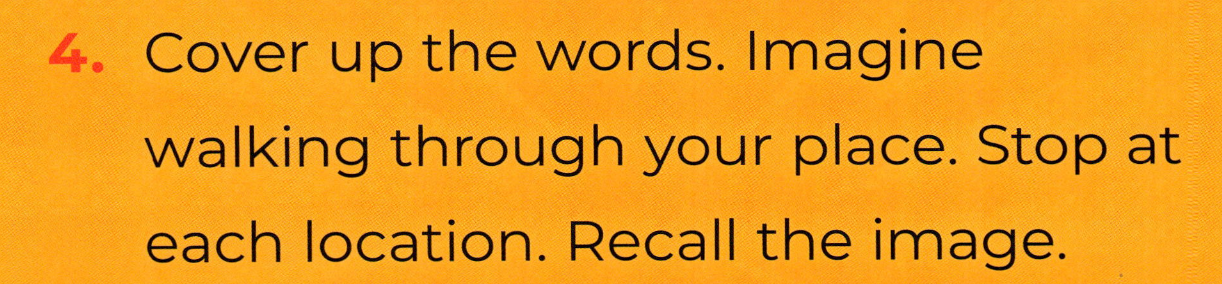

4. Cover up the words. Imagine walking through your place. Stop at each location. Recall the image.

5. Write down the words you remember. Did your memory palace help?

GLOSSARY

amazing—causing wonder or surprise.

athlete—a person who is trained or skilled in sports.

compete— to take part in a contest between two or more persons or groups.

detail—a small part of something larger.

extreme (ihk-STREEM)—far beyond the usual.

information (ihn-fuhr-MAY-shuhn)—knowledge obtained from learning or studying something.

rare—uncommon or not often found or seen.

signal—something that gives warning or a command.

ONLINE RESOURCES

To learn more about superhuman memory, please visit **abdobooklinks.com** or scan this QR code. These links are routinely monitored and updated to provide the most current information available.

INDEX